JADA JONES

★ NATURE LOVER ★

JADA JONES

★ NATURE LOVER ★

by Kelly Starling Lyons
illustrated by Nneka Myers

Penguin Workshop

PENGUIN WORKSHOP
An imprint of Penguin Random House LLC, New York

First published in the United States of America by Penguin Workshop,
an imprint of Penguin Random House LLC, New York, 2022

Text copyright © 2022 by Kelly Starling Lyons
Cover illustration copyright © 2022 by Vanessa Brantley Newton
Illustrations copyright © 2022 by Penguin Random House LLC

PENGUIN is a registered trademark and PENGUIN WORKSHOP is a
trademark of Penguin Books Ltd, and the W colophon is a registered
trademark of Penguin Random House LLC.

Visit us online at penguinrandomhouse.com.

Library of Congress Cataloging-in-Publication Data is available.

Manufactured in China

ISBN 9780593226490 (paperback)   10 9 8 7 6 5 4 3 2 1 LP
ISBN 9780593226506 (library binding)   10 9 8 7 6 5 4 3 2 1 LP

For my grandfather, who loved naming bugs and animals and soaking in nature—KSL

To my family and friends—NM

Chapter One:
READY, SET, POP POP

"Whoa. What's the rush, Jada?" Daddy asked.

I looked down and couldn't believe I'd already gobbled my two supersize banana pancakes.

"They were delicious," I said as I hurried to the sink. I blasted water on my flowered plate and stuck it in the dishwasher. My plate and silverware clattered as I slammed the door shut.

"Careful, Jada," Mom said. "I know you're excited, but you have time. Pop Pop won't arrive for another twenty minutes."

"Sorry," I said, and zipped upstairs to grab the purple backpack I stocked last night.

Water, snacks, journal, and my four-in-one pen for notes. I was all set. Field trip day with Pop Pop! I didn't want to miss a minute.

I raced down the stairs, stuck my paper bag lunch in my backpack, and stood by the door. I couldn't believe Pop Pop was going to be one of our chaperones on the nature trail. I'd finally get to show him off to my friends—and show him what I knew about plants and bugs.

"You get to have all the fun," my little brother, Jackson, said, scrunching his eyebrows as he stood beside me. "Why do you get to take Pop Pop on a field trip and I don't?"

"Bet he'll chaperone your next one," I said. "Just ask him."

I peeked out the window and squealed when I saw Betsy Brown Sugar, Pop Pop's station wagon, pulling up. Right on time.

"He's here!" I yelled to Mom and Dad. I had my hand on the doorknob, about to head out, when I heard Mom's voice.

"Let him come in for a minute," Mom said. "He might want something to eat."

I sighed and shuffled my feet. Felt like forever before he finally came through the door.

"Hey there, Lady Bug," he called when he saw me. His hug was like a cozy blanket.

Jax hung back, poking out his lip.

"Who's this? I know that's not my grandson looking all salty," he said.

Jax cracked a smile and ran over to him. No one can stay mad when Pop Pop is around. He lifted Jax into his arms.

"I know you want to go, too," he said. "We're going to do something special when we get back. Just you and me."

Jax looked at me with a satisfied grin. Now *I was* the one feeling left out.

"You want something to eat, Dad?" Mom asked, kissing his cheek.

"I had a little something something. I think we better get on the road. Right, Lady Bug?"

I smiled and nodded. That's all he needed to say.

"Bye!" I yelled as I rushed out to his car. Time to get this party started.

"Let's see," Pop Pop said, pretending to think through some options. "What should we play on the way?"

"You know."

We always kicked off our drives with the same two songs. Old-school

and new-school versions of "Before I
Let Go." We started with his favorite,
the original by Frankie Beverly
and Maze, and ended with mine, by
Beyoncé.

"So tell me about this nature walk," he said.

"We're going to learn about trees, animals, insects, and plants. There's even a zip line we can ride at the end."

"Now, that's what's up—way up," he said, laughing. "You'll be able to see the whole park. Nothing like looking at nature from overhead. You know I've zip-lined in the islands, in the mountains. You get a different view and appreciation for how wonderful the world is. I can't wait to see you fly."

Way up? I've been on zip lines before at indoor playgrounds. They weren't *that* high. I hoped this one was like those. Pop Pop would be so impressed.

When we pulled up at school, teachers, kids, and chaperones were clustered on the sidewalk near the buses. Some adults sipped from coffee cups. Some kids laughed with friends. Others rubbed their eyes and yawned. I scanned the fourth-grade kids and teachers, searching for my class.

"There's Simone and Lena! You have to meet them," I said, grabbing Pop Pop's hand.

"Hey, Jada," Simone said when we walked up. "Like my look?" She twirled to give a full view of her gray boots dotted with rhinestones and blue camo shirt. Simone has the coolest style. Getting fancy for a trail walk was so her.

"Love it," I said. "This is my Pop Pop. He's coming on the trip with us. He grew up on a farm in West Virginia and knows all about nature. He used to take my mom and Uncle Rob camping. He taught them how to fish and garden. He even used to be a park ranger for a while."

"I don't know everything about

nature," he said, laughing. "But I do love the outdoors."

"I do, too," Lena said. "My mom and I walk at the park near our house every weekend. Sometimes we have a picnic. I wonder if we can sit in the grass and eat lunch today or if we're sitting at tables."

"Picnics are fun," Simone said. Then, she wrinkled her nose. "But nature would be better without all the bugs. Ants, spiders, crickets—they give me the creeps. Butterflies are cool, but everything else has got to go."

I peeked at Pop Pop. I knew he wasn't feeling that. He says every living thing is special and has a purpose. He gives names to each one he sees. Sasha Squirrel. Rory Raccoon. Bakari Bee.

"I see we have some work to do," he said to Simone. "We'll try our best to open your mind. Right, Jada?"

"Yes, sir," I said. I was ready to get started. Operation Show Simone That Nature Is Awesome was on.

We boarded the buses. The adults sat together. I plopped next to Lena, and Simone sat next to Gabi. Miles and RJ were in the row in front of us.

"Did you get the permission slip signed for the zip line?" I heard Simone ask Gabi. "I can't wait. I heard you get to ride from tree to tree."

Zip-lining through the trees? That must have been what Pop Pop was talking about when he said "way up." Suddenly I got that stomach-dropping-to-your-feet feeling that hits when you're about to hop on a super-steep roller coaster.

"You gonna try it, Jada?" Simone turned and asked me.

I was just about to shrug when I caught Pop Pop smiling at me. I bet seeing me on the zip line, soaring like a bird, would make him proud. I took a breath and pushed away my doubts.

"Sure," I said, nodding.

Nothing was going to ruin my day with Pop Pop. Not even my nerves.

Chapter Two:

When we pulled up at the park, our teacher, Miss Taylor, divided us into groups. Lena, Simone, me, Miles, Gabi, and RJ were together. Pop Pop and Mrs. Lewis, Miles's mom, would be our chaperones. Mrs. Lewis is the head of an explorer club Miles belongs to. With her and Pop Pop as our guides, navigating the trail would be a snap.

We each had a worksheet, pencil, and clipboard for the scavenger hunt. We had to try to find the objects and creatures on our paper—bird, flower, bark, lily pad, acorn, spiderweb, moss, nest, and more.

"Okay, everyone, pick a buddy and let's get going," Mrs. Lewis said.

Lena liked nature as much as I did. It would be fun to search with her. But I knew just who my partner should be.

"Simone, want to hunt with me?" I asked.

"Sure," she said. "We're gonna beat everybody."

I looked at Lena and Gabi laughing and Miles and RJ leaning

against a fence, talking.

"I don't think it's a race," I said.
"But you're right, we make a great
team."

We linked arms and headed down
the wooded path.

Pop Pop paused and looked overhead.

"Shhh," he said, facing us and holding a finger to his lips. "Listen."

Our voices shut off like someone flipped a switch. We heard the *cheer, cheer, cheer* of a bird. We looked up at branches, at the rocks and twigs on the ground. Nothing.

"It sounds like someone pushed the remote to find their car," Simone said, giggling.

"Yep," I said. "It's kind of like a whistle, too."

Cheer. Cheer. Cheer.

"Birds can be hard to spot sometimes," Mrs. Lewis whispered, scanning the area to figure out where the call was coming from.

"I see it!" Simone yelled. Her face
lit up as she pointed to a flash of red
in the leaves.

"That's how you do it, Simone,"
Pop Pop said, winking at me.
"Anyone know what kind of bird
that is?"

"A cardinal," she said with pride.

"Nice work, Miss Simone," Pop Pop said. "That's Carl the Cardinal, all right. I think somebody was tricking me about not being into nature."

She looked down and grinned. Not Simone being shy!

"Come on, Jada," she said, grabbing my hand. "What else do we need to find?"

Mushrooms were next on our list. We searched the ground but came up empty. Just when we were ready to move on, we heard Lena.

"Moss!" she called out. "We found moss."

Everyone rushed over to see the green carpet of plants growing on the base of a tree. Lena checked it off on her list.

"Is it true that moss only grows on the north side?" Gabi asked.

I knew the answer to that one. But Lena beat me to it.

"Sometimes it's on the north side," she said. "Sometimes it isn't."

Lena circled the tree.

"See, on this one, it's all the way around. Moisture is what makes it grow."

Pop Pop smiled and nodded. I could tell he was impressed. He volunteers at state parks whenever he can. He loves nature facts.

"Did you know that moss can grow on rocks and soil, too?" I asked Simone.

"Really? That's cool," she said.

I looked around and hoped that Pop Pop was listening. But he was talking to Lena and Gabi. I sighed and waited for my next chance to share what I knew.

Miles and RJ were ahead of the group. I saw them pointing at something out of view.

"Come on back, boys," Mrs. Lewis said.

"Can we go to the pond, Mom?"

Miles asked. "The sign says it's right around the bend."

"Okay," Mrs. Lewis said, "before we get there, what are we looking for?"

We studied our papers and rattled off the items. Then we rushed down the trail and headed for the wooden footbridge. We lined the railing and peered at the green water.

"Look at that turtle," Miles said.

It was gliding on the surface with its legs spread out and brown shell glistening. As we gazed around us, we found everything we needed. Lily pad. Fish. Ducks. They were all here.

A dragonfly lingered nearby before zipping across the pond. Its lacy wings sparkled in the light.

"What do we know about dragonflies?" Mrs. Lewis asked.

"They're great at flying," Miles answered in a flash.

"That's right," Pop Pop said. "They're fast, strong fliers that can hover, fly straight and backward, sideways, up and down."

"Who knows how long dragonflies

have been around?"

"Millions of years," Gabi said, beating me to it. I wondered if I was ever going to get the chance to show Pop Pop that nature was my thing and I had skills.

We soaked in the sunshine and watched it gleam on the mirror of the pond.

"This is so pretty," Simone said. "I could stand here all day."

Pop Pop was right. Simone was turning into a nature lover after all. Once we crossed the bridge, we entered the other side of the shady trail. Leafy branches formed a canopy above us. The path began to narrow so that we had to go one by one.

"Bet we can find the next thing before anyone else," Simone said to me.

She steamed ahead without looking where she was going.

"Ew! Get it off me! Get it off me!" she said, wiping her face frantically.

"What is it, Simone?!" I said.

"A spiderweb," Miles said, pointing to the leftover strands. "A humongous one."

We tried to help Simone brush it off. But she wouldn't stay still. She was pawing at her face, raking her fingers through her hair. I loved being outside, but even I didn't like the way the threads of a web cling to you and feel like they're everywhere. I didn't blame her for freaking out.

"I told you I don't like bugs," she said, groaning.

I didn't bother telling her that spiders are arachnids. Everything was going so well. Why did she have to run into that web?

That made me think of something.
I glanced at my clipboard.

"Simone, you did it! Spiderweb
was on the list. And guess what? You
definitely found it first."

I hoped that would make her
laugh. She didn't crack a smile.

Pop Pop came over to check on her.

"Simone, I know spiderwebs can feel funny when you walk into them," he said. "But they're pretty amazing. What do we know about them?"

Finally, my chance to shine.

"Spiderwebs are five times stronger than steel," Gabi said. "We can walk through them because they're really thin. But if they were thick like a metal beam, forget about it."

Pop Pop's eyes lit up, and he laughed. I scanned my brain for facts.

"They're made of silk," Miles said.

"They're sticky so they can catch their prey," RJ said.

Oh no. That was what I was going to say. I knew a lot about webs. Why couldn't I think of anything to add? I looked at Pop Pop beaming at my friends and thought as hard as I could. Nothing. It was like someone hit the clear button on my brain.

"I don't think you kids need us," Mrs. Lewis said. "You got it covered."

"Yep, you're naturals," Pop Pop chimed in.

Naturals? Not me. Why did I feel like I was letting Simone and Pop Pop down?

Chapter Three:
PRICKLY SITUATION

For the next part of our hike, we took out our journals and fanned across a field. We were going to draw pictures of some of the plants we saw. I pulled out my four-in-one pen so I'd have a choice of colors. Mrs. Lewis said there were hundreds of varieties of plants on the grounds.

"Make sure you look with your eyes and not your hands," she said. "Safety first. Some plants are delicate. Others have ways of protecting themselves. We'll have a time where you can feel things later on."

"Remember to use your sense of smell, too," Pop Pop said. "Sweet, minty, earthy, and even stinky, what does the plant's odor remind you of? As you're looking at the plants, do you see any insects? Draw pictures and take notes about those, too."

Bugs. Uh-oh. Simone frowned when he mentioned that. I looked around. Gold-and-purple wildflowers painted the ground with pops of color. I bet she'd love those.

"Why don't we start over here?"
I said.

Simone walked slowly, but I saw her eyes brighten as she checked them out. We sat next to each other on the ground and drew the stems and the leaves. Simone took her time with the petals, getting the shape, shading, and texture just right. I didn't know she was such a good artist.

Buzz. Buzz. I heard it before I saw it. A bee started flying around us. It circled my head. I stayed still, and it left. When it buzzed near Simone, she swatted. It zoomed away and then came back for more.

"Don't move around so much, Simone," I said. "It will probably go if you leave it alone or back away slowly."

Simone was not having it. She stood, waved her arms, and

swung her notebook.

She lost her grip, and the journal flew into some weeds.

"Oh no!" she said.

"I'll get it," I said.

I carefully stepped into the plants and reached to grab her notebook.

"Ow!"

Prickers. I gave Simone the notebook and saw drops of blood on my fingertip. Not a lot, but it stung.

"Mr. Moyer," Simone said, rushing over to Pop Pop. "Jada's hurt."

"Let me see, Lady Bug," he said, taking my hand and looking at it closely. "It's not that bad."

He got out the first aid kit, cleaned the cut, and put a Band-Aid on it as everyone watched what was happening.

"Thanks, Pop Pop," I said, and looked down at the ground. I was supposed to be showing him what I can do. Some nature girl.

"Thanks for getting my notebook for me, Jada," Simone said. "Sorry you cut your finger."

"I'm okay," I said. "It was just my pride that got hurt."

Simone laughed. I did, too. I was glad she was feeling better. We only had one more stop before lunch—the nature center. What else could go wrong?

As we walked to the low beige building with rocking chairs in the front, I heard a whizzing sound and spotted a girl from another class grinning as she sailed down the zip line. A spark raced through me like excitement mixed with the jitters.

"Whoa! That's so cool. Are you trying it, RJ?" Miles asked.

"Naw, not me," he said, looking up and shaking his head. "I'm staying right here on the ground. You?"

"Definitely."

Simone started cheesing like crazy and did a dance.

"Did you see that?"

Gabi high-fived Simone. She was psyched, too.

"That's what I'm talking about, Jada," Simone said. "That's going to be us."

Us? My stomach did a backflip. I wasn't sure about that. It looked fun, but it was way higher than ones I had been on before. I didn't know if I could do it.

Pop Pop saw the zip line, too. His eyes twinkled as he gave me a thumbs-up. I did one back and swallowed hard.

Chapter Four:
A Different View

I nside the center, there were touch stations and displays about some of the plants and flowers we saw. Glass boxes and habitats gave us close-up views of a few of the animals and insects that lived at the park, too.

I remembered Simone saying she liked butterflies. I pulled her over to watch a caterpillar inch along a branch.

"It looks creepy," she said, staring at its long, striped yellow, white, and black body, "but kinda cool."

There was a wall that showed the stages of the caterpillar transforming into a green chrysalis and emerging as an orange monarch butterfly.

"We can't have one without the other," I said.

"Yeah, I guess you're right."

"Jada and Simone, check this out," Lena called.

She and Gabi were standing in front of a clear wall that showed the inside of an anthill. Simone frowned but came along. We watched streams of ants moving through the dirt passages like soldiers in a row.

"Can you believe they all have jobs?" Lena said.

Facts were written on a panel near the exhibit: Ants can lift fifty times their body weight. There are thousands of kinds of ants—carpenter ants, fire ants, acrobat ants, and more.

"Acrobat ants?" Simone said. "Now, that's *my* kind of bug. Do they cartwheel and do back handsprings? Can they double Dutch?"

I laughed, thinking about ants doing our favorite sport. I pictured them twirling tiny ropes and nailing tricks. They could donkey kick, cartwheel, do it all.

"If there was a double Dutching

ant, would you let it on your team?"
I asked Simone.

"For sure," she said without missing a beat. "If it could jump."

We cracked up. That's Simone.

The next section focused on flowers. There were so many different kinds. Black-eyed Susans, lilies, magnolia blossoms, snapdragons . . . The list went on and on.

"Look at the colors," Lena said. "It's like a rainbow."

Nearby there was a model of a hive and a sign that described why bees are so important. They're pollinators that make it possible for plants to grow and create food.

"I didn't know all that," Simone said.

She actually looked interested instead of grossed out.

"Okay, girls," Mrs. Lewis said as

she walked over. "It's time for lunch."

We left the center and joined the other students in our class. Miles and RJ sat at a picnic table with Pop Pop holding our spots.

Just when we pulled out our lunches and started munching, we heard RJ groan.

"Ugh, ants!"

A trio of ants crept along the top of the table. He brushed them away. Looked like Simone wasn't the only one who was bugged by bugs. But the funny thing was, Simone kept eating and didn't flinch.

"What kind of ants do you think those are?" I asked her.

"Greedy ones," she said, laughing.

Pop Pop's eyes sparkled.

"Yep, old Antwan Ant and his crew are ready to eat just like we are," he said. "Okay, Miss Simone, I have to ask. Do you feel the same way about bugs as when you came?"

"They're not my favorites, but I guess they're not all bad."

"Is that so?" he said, winking at me. "We'll take it. Right, Lady Bug?"

I nodded and felt warm all over like when the field trip started. Things were finally turning around. As we cleaned up, Miss Taylor asked everyone who was going zip-lining to gather together.

My stomach dropped. Just when I was back on track, my thoughts started racing again.

I wanted Pop Pop to be proud. If I rode it, I could tell him all about what the park looked like from way up there. Pop Pop has zip-lined over a waterfall in Jamaica. This was easy compared to that. The girl I saw riding looked like she was having a blast. I could, too. Try it or pass?

"Finally, it's time for the best part," Simone said, bouncing in her seat.

My heart thumped like it was playing drums in a marching band. I was getting queasy just thinking about going up there. What was I going to do?

Chapter Five:
THE CLIMB

Miss Taylor said anyone who
didn't want to zip-line could
learn about the animals
of the park and even meet a few.
There were otters, frogs, snakes.
Lena and RJ were down for that.
I wondered if I should go, too. I
kinda wanted to try the zip line,
but I kept thinking about how high
we had to climb.

"Come on, Jada," Simone said. "We can go right after each other."

I stared at the towering trunks and leafy ceiling above us. Those trees looked like skyscrapers. Was I really doing this?

"You go ahead, Simone," I said. "I'll catch up."

She ran over to Gabi and Miles.

"What's wrong, Lady Bug?" Pop Pop asked.

"Nothing."

"You can't fool me," he said. "I see how you're looking at that zip line. It's okay if you're nervous. Only do it if you really want to."

At first, I wanted to ride it to show Pop Pop that I was daring and a nature lover like him, but now I wanted to do it for me. I inhaled and decided to give it a try.

"I'm going," I said. "Wish me luck."

"You don't need it," Pop Pop said. "You know why I call you Lady Bug?"

"Because I'm cute," I said, tilting my head and smiling.

"That too," he said, laughing. "But ladybugs bring luck wherever they go. You don't need to wish for something that's already part of you."

As I walked over, Simone waved to me to hurry.

"I thought you'd never get here," she said. "Let's go."

Every step closer to getting a harness for the zip line made that queasy feeling in my stomach get stronger. I felt like I was on a ship and it was rocking back and forth. I grabbed one of my braids and twirled it around my finger and untwirled it. Twirl and untwirl.

I'd been on zip lines before. This one was just higher. I knew I could do it, even if my legs weren't so sure.

I watched Miles and Gabi put on their harnesses. They climbed to the platform at the top smooth and steady.

Then it was Simone's turn. In a flash, she had on the gear and was halfway there. She turned and grinned at me over her shoulder. I was up.

I stepped inside the loops for my legs and feel the belt and buckles tighten around me. I put on my helmet. The helper made sure everything was secure. It was time to climb.

I focused and took it one step at a time. *Don't look down. Don't look down*, I told myself. I breathed and kept going.

Finally, I was on the platform.
I saw Simone getting ready to ride.

Then what did I do? I looked down.
Pop Pop and Mrs. Lewis waved at
me. They looked like action figures
instead of full-size people.
Cars in the parking lot looked as
tiny as toys. Everything was so far
away from way up here. I felt dizzy.
Then I couldn't move. It was like I
was glued to my spot.

I knew someone was talking, but
I couldn't tell what they were saying
at first. All I heard was my breath
coming quicker and quicker. Then,
slowly, I made out the words.

"Jada, are you okay?" Simone
called.

I nodded.

"You got this," she said. "Watch me."

In a whoosh, she soared down the line. She kicked her legs and whooped.

"Do you still want to ride?" the attendant asked.

I inhaled and stood up tall. No more stalling.

"I'm ready," I said, finding my voice.

I stepped forward. It was time to fly.

Chapter Six

UP, UP, AND AWAY

I closed my eyes when my feet left the platform. I heard the whirr of the zip line and felt wind rushing across my face. I opened my eyes and—wow. It was like I was a falcon gliding over the whole park. I could see the bridge, the pond, the flowers, the nature center, green fields that stretched for miles. Pop Pop was right. I would never forget this view.

I relaxed and breathed in the
sweet smell of sunshine mixed
with pine. I leaned back as the park
zoomed by. Before I knew it, the ride
was over. I wished I could do it again
and again.

When I came down, Simone, Gabi,
and Miles were waiting with Pop
Pop and Mrs. Lewis. High fives all
around.

"You did it!" Simone said. "Wasn't
that amazing?"

Pop Pop gave me a hug.

"That's my Lady Bug," he said.

Tired and happy, we plopped
down in the rocking chairs at the
nature center.

I saw Simone staring at something:
a spider scrambling on its web. Uh-oh.
I knew how she felt about them.

"You want to go somewhere else?"
I asked.

"No, I'm okay," she said. Simone
stopped watching it and kept
rocking. We talked about our
favorite parts of the trip. The zip
line was number one for both of us.
Simone surprised me by saying that
the footbridge over the pond and
walking through the woods were
special, too.

"You showed me some cool stuff
today, Jada," she said. "Thanks."

I looked up and caught Pop
Pop smiling at us. He didn't have
to tell me he was proud. I could
feel it.

Simone sucked her teeth when it

was time to board the buses.

"Dang," she said. "I wish we had more time."

"Me too," Lena said. "Our group got to touch a snake. It felt warm and smooth, not slimy at all like I thought it would."

I sat next to Simone on the way back.

"Think you want to come here again?" I asked her.

"Definitely," she said.

"Even with the bugs?"

"Bugs got nothing on me," she said, and struck a pose in her seat.

Simone was back.

At school, we hugged and got ready to head home. RJ was already thinking about the next field trip.

"Miss Taylor, how about the beach?" RJ said. "Can we go there next?"

"Yeah, the beach would be awesome," Miles said.

"What about the mountains?" Lena said.

"We'll see, kids," she said, laughing. "One field trip at a time."

Chapter Seven:
JUST YOU AND ME

On the way home, Pop Pop didn't put on our songs right away.

"I'm proud of you," he said, "not because you rode the zip line. I would have been just as proud if you passed. I'm proud because you wanted to do something, and even though you were nervous, you kept going. We're all afraid sometimes. It's how we deal with the fear that counts."

I thought about feeling dizzy and then freezing on the platform.

"When I was up there, I almost came back down. But I knew I could do it."

"I did, too."

Pop Pop hit the music. We sang along to "Before I Let Go" and jammed in our seats.

When we got to my house, no one was there. Dad takes Jax to karate class after school on Fridays. Mom gets home later.

"Okay, I promised your brother something special," Pop Pop said when we stepped inside. "Any ideas?"

"Hmmm. He likes cars, *Star Wars* toys, building with Magna-Tiles.

But he plays with those all the time."

Then I thought about our day at the park, and it came to me. I knew just what he'd love.

"I've got it," I said. "Follow me."

We walked down to the basement and pulled out the tent I used on my Girl Scout trips.

"We can set it up in the backyard," I said.

We put sleeping bags in the tent and made a campsite just for them. When we were done, I checked the kitchen cabinet and pulled out graham crackers, chocolate squares, and marshmallows. All set.

Pop Pop and I played Uno and chess until Jax and Dad came in.

"Pop Pop!"

He ran over for a hug.

"Ranger Jax, are you ready?" he asked.

"Ready for what?"

"Camp Pop Pop is in session. Just you and me. Run upstairs and get changed. I'll meet you outside."

Daddy grinned.

"Backyard camping?" he teased.

"You always bring it. Keisha and I have to get more creative."

"I can't take the credit," he said. "This was all Miss Lady Bug's idea."

"Have a good time," I said, giving Pop Pop a hug and then heading up to my room. I took out my nature journal and looked over my drawings and notes. I thought about how

Simone and I faced our fears. I'd remember our trip for a long time.

A few minutes later, Jax popped his head in.

"You want to come camping with Pop Pop and me?"

"Thanks, Jax," I said. "But that's okay. I had Pop Pop to myself. Now you get to have time with him, too."

He paused for a minute like he was thinking it over.

"I want you to come out with us," he said. "It's not the same without you."

Sometimes Jax surprised me. I smiled and grabbed my sleeping bag. In our tent, we took turns telling stories. Pop Pop shared one

of his favorite tales about Anansi
the Spider, a Ghanaian folklore hero
and trickster god. I bet Simone would
love him.

We ate s'mores and listened to crickets and frogs sing. Above us stars twinkled like a string of lights. I looked at the world around me and then at Jax and Pop Pop. Nature was amazing, especially when you shared it with people you loved.

JADA'S RULES FOR BEING A NATURE LOVER

1. Breathe in the scents around you.

2. Soak in the sounds.

3. Keep your eyes and mind open.

4. Be curious and careful.

5. Enjoy nature with someone special.

ACKNOWLEDGMENTS

Writing the Jada Jones series fills me with joy. I'm so touched by young readers who share that they connect with Jada and her friends or that a book in the series inspired them to believe in the power they hold inside.

You've heard about Jada's grandfather in earlier books. I couldn't wait to feature him in this one. Pop Pop was inspired by my maternal granddad, who grew up in West Virginia and loved nature just like Jada's grandfather. My granddad took us fishing at Lake Erie, showed us the wonder of space through a telescope, made us food that came from his garden. Beauty is all around, he would say. You just have to look.

A couple of cherished memories are sitting with him and my grandma on the porch as lightning bugs flickered in the night. I also loved the names he gave animals and bugs he saw. Rory Raccoon was one of my favorites.

Thank you to people like my grandparents and groups like Outdoor Afro and the National Wildlife Federation that connect kids with nature. Looking for things to do? Make mud pies and bird-watch with friends, walk a park trail with loved ones and have a picnic, splash in the waves at the beach. Be safe and have fun.

I'm grateful, as always, to my editor Renee, the amazing team at Penguin Workshop, illustrators Nneka Myers and Vanessa Brantley Newton, and my agent Caryn Wiseman, for making this book possible. Thanks, too, to my family and friends, my sorors, Brown Bookshelf fam, Novelette sisters, and Quint fam who celebrate each new book and cheer me on.